Welcome to
The Giggle Club

The Giggle Club is a collection of picture books made to put a giggle into early reading. There are funny stories about a contrary mouse, a dancing fox, a turtle with a trumpet, a pig with a ball, a hungry monster, a laughing lobster, an elephant who sneezes away the jungle and lots more! Each of these characters is a member of **The Giggle Club**, but anyone can join: just pick up a **Giggle Club** book, read it and get giggling!

Turn to the checklist on the inside back cover and tick off the Giggle Club books you have read.

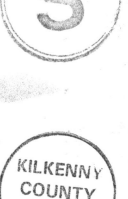

TEE HEE!

HA HA!

For David

First published 1996 by Walker Books Ltd
87 Vauxhall Walk, London SE11 5HJ

This edition published 1997

10 9 8 7 6 5

© 1996 Colin West

This book has been typeset in Plantin.

Printed in Hong Kong

British Library Cataloguing in Publication Data
A catalogue record for this book
is available from the British Library.

ISBN 0-7445-5279-6

"I DON'T CARE!" SAID THE BEAR

COLIN WEST

WALKER BOOKS
AND SUBSIDIARIES
LONDON • BOSTON • SYDNEY

"There's a moose on the loose!"
said the teeny-weeny mouse.

"I don't care," said the bear,
with his nose in the air.

"There's a moose on the loose and a bad-tempered goose!" said the teeny-weeny mouse.

"I don't care," said the bear,
with his nose in the air.

"There's a moose on the loose
and a bad-tempered goose
and a pig who is big!"
said the teeny-weeny mouse.

"I don't care," said the bear,
with his nose in the air.

KK199026

"There's a moose on the loose
 and a bad-tempered goose
 and a pig who is big
 and a snake from a lake!"
said the teeny-weeny mouse.

"I don't care," said the bear,
with his nose in the air.

"There's a moose on the loose
and a bad-tempered goose
and a pig who is big
and a snake from a lake
and a wolf from the north!"
said the teeny-weeny mouse.

"I don't care!" said the bear,
with his nose in the air.

"There's a moose on the loose
and a bad-tempered goose
and a pig who is big
and a snake from a lake
and a wolf from the north
and a teeny-weeny mouse!"
said the teeny-weeny mouse.

"YIKES!" said the bear.
And he leapt in the air!

Then that great big old bear ran off back to his lair.